SCENE OF THE CRIME SCENE OF THE CRIME
SCENE OF THE CRIME NE OF THE CRIME

DEATH COMES TO DINNER

MARVIN · MILLER

Illustrated by Robert Roper

SCHOLASTIC INC.
New York Toronto London Auckland Sydney

ISBN 0-590-56871-X

Text copyright © 1995 by Marvin Miller. Illustrations copyright © 1995 by Scholastic Inc. All rights reserved. Published by Scholastic Inc.

12 11 10 9 8 7 6 5 4 3 2 1   5 6 7 8 9/9 0/0

Printed in the U.S.A.   40

First Scholastic printing, August 1995

Also by Marvin Miller:

You Be the Jury
You Be the Jury: Courtroom II
You Be the Jury: Courtroom III
You Be the Jury: Courtroom IV
You Be the Detective
You Be the Detective II
Who Dunnit?
The Mad Scientist's Secret

For Randy, Audrey, and Greg

Contents

Scene of the Crime

How WOULD YOU LIKE TO BE A DETECtive? If you think it would be fun, then meet Sherwood Hawk. He is the sharpest detective in Fernwell.

No matter how tough the case, Hawk manages to solve it. When he arrives at the scene of the crime, he has an amazing talent for finding the right clue that cracks the case.

In this SCENE OF THE CRIME book, you can match wits with Sherwood Hawk. There are ten cases for you to solve.

And you can test your own detective skills by keeping track of the number of clues you need to help you solve the case. IT IS JUST LIKE A GAME WITH POINTS AND SCORES! Just follow the directions after each story.

Here is how it works:

First, read the story carefully. Look for a clue in the illustration of the scene of the crime. Do you think you solved the case?

After you think you know the answer, turn the page. At the end of each story are four clues.

One of them was used by Sherwood Hawk. Which one was it?

Pick the one that you think Hawk used. *But don't look at the solution just yet.*

After you have picked a clue, follow the coded instructions underneath it. (Simply read the letters backward, from right to left.) They will tell you if you are hot on the trail. But if you selected the wrong clue, you can choose another.

After you have the right clue, try to solve the mystery!

Now you can turn to the SOLUTION page. Did you solve the case?

Following each solution is a SCORING page. Figure out your score for the case.

On page 83 of this book you can list *all* your scores and add up the total.

The final score tells you how good a detective you are.

So put on your thinking cap and get to work. Sherwood Hawk is waiting for you — at the scene of the crime.

DEATH COMES TO DINNER

Death Comes to Dinner

HORACE HUBBLE LOOKED DOWN UN-
easily at the sprawled-out figure on his restaurant floor. Detective Sherwood Hawk was standing next to him.

"I was in the kitchen when Ed Kane was mur-
dered!" Hubble stammered.

As the body was removed to a waiting police
van, a glum Hawk looked on. Then he glanced
across the room at two bullet holes in the glass
door. "Did you hear any gunshots?" asked Hawk.

The owner slowly nodded. "I did hear a shot
ring out. And a few seconds later, I heard a second one. I dashed out of the kitchen and there
was Kane, lying on the floor."

Hawk walked over to the door and examined
the bullet holes. The indentation of the upper
hole proved the bullet was fired from inside the
dining room. The lower hole was made by a shot
fired from outside.

"The murderer must have aimed at Kane
right through the glass," said Hawk. Then the
detective opened the door and began searching
the outside of the restaurant.

Suddenly Hawk noticed a pair of steel-rimmed
glasses lying on the ground. Maybe they were

dropped by the murderer. He picked them up and returned to Hubble.

Hawk examined the glasses carefully. "I'd say these belong to a man about five feet eight inches tall. The width of the glasses tells me his head size, and from that I can guess his height. Judging from the spread of the nosepiece, he has a narrow nose."

The detective pointed to a small spot of green tarnish on the rim. "See this mark? It usually comes from salt air. The person who owns these probably does a lot of boating or fishing."

"That describes Sam Smit!" exclaimed a surprised Hubble. "Smit and Kane used to be friends. Smit rents a room down the street."

Hawk turned to a police sergeant. "See if you can find Smit," he ordered. "I have more questions for Hubble."

When the policeman departed, Hubble continued. "Kane came in for dinner before the rush-hour crowd. He had just been released from jail on Monday. I guess he wanted to celebrate."

"What was he jailed for?" asked Hawk.

"Bank robbery," replied Hubble. "Kane and his partner Smit were both convicted of robbing the Fernwell Bank. Smit was arrested first. The next day the police tracked down Kane. Kane thought that Smit had squealed on him."

As Hawk examined the crime scene, the policeman returned, gripping Sam Smit's arm.

3

Smit tried to shake loose. "How did you figure out it was me?" he asked in an agitated voice.

Hawk waved the glasses. "Are these yours?"

"Sure they are," Smit said. "They must have fallen out of my pocket after I shot Kane."

"Then I arrest you for the murder of Ed Kane," announced Hawk.

"But I shot him in self-defense!" shrieked Smit. "Kane fired at me first."

"What do you mean?" asked a skeptical Hawk.

"Kane thought I double-crossed him. He swore he would get even after we got out of jail."

Smit anxiously continued. "I didn't know Kane was eating here. When I came up to the restaurant, Kane spotted me. He pulled out a gun and fired. But the bullet whizzed by my head.

"Lucky I had my pistol. I fired back through the glass door."

"How do I know that you didn't shoot first?" asked Hawk suspiciously. "Maybe Kane returned your fire to defend himself."

"You've got to believe me," pleaded Smit.

Hawk again surveyed the crime scene and then turned to Smit. "You know? I'm beginning to believe your story. In fact, I am certain I can convince a jury you fired in self-defense."

HOW DID HAWK KNOW? TRY TO SOLVE THE MYSTERY; THEN TURN TO THE NEXT PAGE.

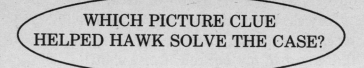

WHICH PICTURE CLUE HELPED HAWK SOLVE THE CASE?

A. thgir ton si siht tub dab oot

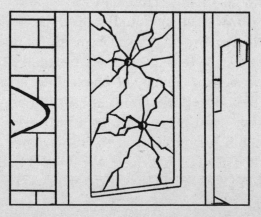

B. esac eht evlos ot eciohc tcefrep a

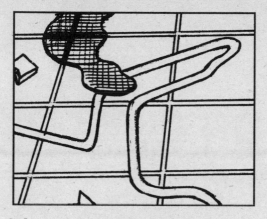

C. daetsni esle gnihtemos nwod kcart

D. ti evlos pleh ot ereh gnihton

AFTER YOU HAVE CHOSEN THE RIGHT
CLUE, TRY TO SOLVE THE MYSTERY.
THEN TURN TO THE SOLUTION TO SEE IF
YOU FIGURED IT OUT.

SOLUTION

When Hawk examined the top bullet hole (fired by Kane), he noticed it branched out in all directions. But some of the cracks from the second bullet (fired by Smit) were stopped from spreading.

A crack that is made first will stop the spread of one made after it. The second crack would run until it met the first.

This proves that the top bullet hole was made before the bottom one.

With this evidence, Hawk knew he could prove that Smit fired in self-defense.

SCORING

If you picked the correct clue
immediately, score 3 points.

If you needed TWO clues, score 2 points.

If you needed THREE clues, score 1 point.

If you needed FOUR clues, score 0 points.

POINTS_____

DID YOU SOLVE THE CASE?
IF YOU DID, SCORE 3 POINTS.

POINTS_____

IF YOU CRACKED THE CASE *BEFORE*
YOU LOOKED AT THE CLUE PAGES,
ADD AN EXTRA 4 POINTS.

POINTS_____

TOTAL SCORE
CASE #1_____

The Redheaded Robber

DETECTIVE SHERWOOD HAWK GLANCED at his watch as he entered the Quick-Stop Grocery Store. It was ten-thirty in the morning. Greg Perkins was standing behind the checkout counter. He looked slightly dazed.

"You came just in time," exclaimed Perkins. "I've been robbed! There was more than five hundred dollars in my cash register."

Perkins caught his breath. "A man came into my store just fifteen minutes ago. He wore a mask and his hand was in his pocket. He said he had a gun and forced me to open the register."

Hawk frowned. "Can you describe what he looked like?"

"Not very well," answered Perkins. "The man was wearing a baseball cap and zipped-up jacket. But I did notice a wisp of red hair."

Hawk stroked his chin. He was deep in concentration. Then he looked up at Perkins. "Was he wearing a full mask over his entire face?"

"How did you know?" replied a startled Perkins.

"It just might be Arthur Tripp," said Hawk thoughtfully. "We brought him to police headquarters for questioning last week. It was about another robbery. But there wasn't enough evidence to hold him."

"But what does that have to do with the mask?" asked Perkins.

"Tripp is a redhead and he also has a scar on his right cheek. So he would need a full face mask to cover the scar."

Perkins listened in amazement as Hawk turned toward the door. "I think I will pay Tripp a visit. He lives on Sterling Avenue, less than a mile from here." Then Hawk exited the grocery, leaving a bewildered Perkins behind.

Sterling Avenue was a tree-lined street nestled behind the town's soccer field. As Hawk drove by, he recognized a redbrick house with white shutters. The grass had not been mowed for weeks.

Hawk knocked on Tripp's door. No answer. Hawk knocked again, this time much harder.

As Hawk patiently waited, the door slowly opened. A sleepy-looking man with red hair peered at the detective through half-closed eyes.

"More questions?" mumbled Arthur Tripp. "I answered them all at headquarters last week."

Hawk stepped inside as Tripp plopped into a chair.

"Excuse me if I sit down," Tripp said groggily. "I had a poker game here last evening. It lasted past midnight."

"I'm here about something different," said

Hawk. "There was a holdup at the Quick-Stop Grocery not more than twenty minutes ago."

Tripp stiffened. He gave Hawk a strange look. "What does that have to do with me?"

"Where were you this morning between ten and ten-thirty?" Hawk asked as he glanced at the scar on Tripp's right cheek.

Tripp jumped up. "Surely you don't suspect me? I've been in the house all morning. I never went out."

The man paused and then continued. "In fact, I was stretched out on the couch for a nap. I dozed off for a few hours. You woke me when you knocked."

Hawk gazed around the neat room. "I see you cleaned up after the card game."

"That's why I didn't get to bed until two," blurted Tripp.

Hawk studied the tired face of Tripp, wondering if he was telling the truth. Then he gave him a hardened stare. "I think you'd better accompany me to police headquarters."

"But why?" replied Tripp. "I told you I was here all morning."

"I doubt that," said Hawk sternly. "I have reason to believe you were the masked robber."

HOW DID HAWK KNOW? TRY TO SOLVE THE MYSTERY; THEN TURN TO THE NEXT PAGE.

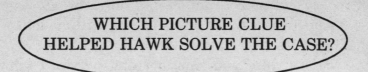

WHICH PICTURE CLUE HELPED HAWK SOLVE THE CASE?

A. gnikool no peek rewsna gnorw

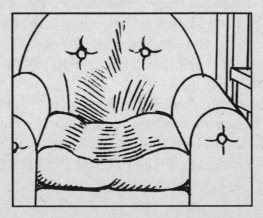

B. eulc eht evah uoy krow ecin

C. redrah hcraes eciohc nekatsim

D. tcerroc ton si eulc eht tub yrros

AFTER YOU HAVE CHOSEN THE RIGHT CLUE, TRY TO SOLVE THE MYSTERY. THEN TURN TO THE SOLUTION TO SEE IF YOU FIGURED IT OUT.

SOLUTION

As Tripp was explaining that he was in the house all morning, Hawk noticed the chair he had just sat in. The cushion was indented.

But the cushions on the couch were all plumped up. If Tripp had been napping on the couch when Hawk knocked on the door, its cushions would have been crushed in, too.

When Hawk pointed out the smooth couch cushions, Tripp admitted he had pretended he was napping to make up an alibi.

He broke down and confessed to the Quick-Stop robbery.

SCORING

If you picked the correct clue
immediately, score 3 points.

If you needed TWO clues, score 2 points.

If you needed THREE clues, score 1 point.

If you needed FOUR clues, score 0 points.

POINTS_____

DID YOU SOLVE THE CASE?
IF YOU DID, SCORE 3 POINTS.

POINTS_____

IF YOU CRACKED THE CASE *BEFORE*
YOU LOOKED AT THE CLUE PAGES,
ADD AN EXTRA 4 POINTS.

POINTS_____

TOTAL SCORE
CASE #2_____

The Accident on the 10:04

DETECTIVE SHERWOOD HAWK WAS standing on the platform of the Fernwell train station waiting for the 10:04 to arrive.

As he whiffed the aroma of fresh popcorn drifting from a nearby snack stand, Hawk walked over to buy a bag. Just then, a rumbling sound signaled that the train was about to arrive.

"I'm in luck," said Hawk to Jillian, the clerk. "I should get a seat. It won't be very crowded."

Jillian gave Hawk a curious look. "But how do you know?"

Hawk smiled. "I can feel its vibrations. The platform is shaking more than usual. That happens when the train has more cars."

"So then it won't be very crowded," replied Jillian, following Hawk's reasoning. She looked up as the train began to pull into the station.

"You're right!" Jillian exclaimed in surprise. "There are three extra cars."

As the train approached, suddenly a stray dog leaped off the long platform and onto the tracks.

"Stop!" Hawk shouted. His voice barely could be heard above the screech of braking wheels. The train came to a stop just in front of the dog.

As the detective hurried into the front car, a

worried engineer rushed out of his cabin. "I slammed on the brakes just in time. It's a good thing I didn't hit that crazy dog."

Suddenly Hawk stiffened. "We'd better make sure that no one was hurt."

When Hawk entered the next car, he saw a man sprawled on the floor between the seats. He was lying on his back, motionless. A magazine was next to him.

"Are you all right?" the detective asked.

The man didn't answer. Hawk quickly bent down and rolled up the man's sleeve.

"What are you doing?" asked the engineer.

"I just want to see if he is unconscious. If I squeeze his upper arm and he doesn't flinch, that is a sure sign he blacked out."

Before Hawk could pinch him, the man suddenly opened his eyes. "My head," he murmured. "I fell back and hit my head."

"Don't try to move," warned Hawk. "How did it happen?"

The man answered in a weak voice. "I got up from my seat to walk toward the front car. Then the train braked suddenly. It threw me to the floor."

Hawk carefully felt the back of the passenger's head. "Ouch!" cried the man. "Now my neck hurts, too. Everything looks blurry."

Hawk began to pull down the passenger's rolled-up sleeve. "Don't touch me!" the man

19

shouted, his voice growing stronger. "I want a lawyer. These trains are not safe."

The man pointed a finger at the engineer. "Don't you even know how to slow down your own train? It's all *your* fault!"

Hawk tried to calm the passenger, but he was brushed away. "When I get out of here, I'm going to see my lawyer," said the man. "I'll sue this railroad for every dollar it has."

He took a deep breath. "A concussion. That's what I have, a concussion. I may have to be in bed for weeks. Get me a doctor. The train company is going to pay for this!"

The engineer looked helplessly at the man lying on the floor. The accident could cost him his job.

Hawk stood up and stared at the passenger. "Quiet down. I'm sure you'll be okay. You're not hurt as badly as you want us to believe."

The man lay motionless and gave Hawk a confused look.

"And forget about the idea of a lawsuit," snapped the detective. "I think you're just faking the accident to collect money for your injury."

HOW DID HAWK KNOW? TRY TO SOLVE THE MYSTERY; THEN TURN TO THE NEXT PAGE.

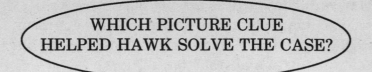

WHICH PICTURE CLUE
HELPED HAWK SOLVE THE CASE?

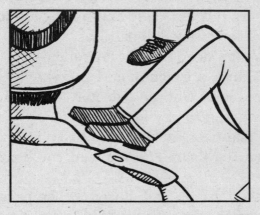

A. eulc tcerroc eht si noitceles ruoy

B. redrah kool doog on tub yrt ecin

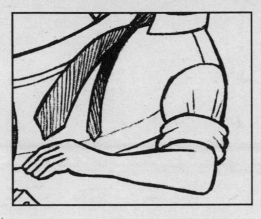

C. siht no esolc neve ton era uoy

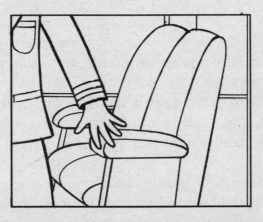

D. eno gnorw eht esohc uoy tub yrros

AFTER YOU HAVE CHOSEN THE RIGHT
CLUE, TRY TO SOLVE THE MYSTERY.
THEN TURN TO THE SOLUTION TO SEE IF
YOU FIGURED IT OUT.

SOLUTION

The passenger said he was walking toward the front car when the sudden stop of the train threw him to the floor. If this had happened, the man would have been thrown *forward* on his stomach, not backward.

But Hawk saw that the man's head was toward the rear of the train and his feet toward the front. The accident had to be a fake.

When Hawk confronted the passenger with this evidence, the man meekly stood up and hurried off the train.

SCORING

If you picked the correct clue
immediately, score 3 points.

If you needed TWO clues, score 2 points.

If you needed THREE clues, score 1 point.

If you needed FOUR clues, score 0 points.

POINTS_____

DID YOU SOLVE THE CASE?
IF YOU DID, SCORE 3 POINTS.

POINTS_____

IF YOU CRACKED THE CASE *BEFORE*
YOU LOOKED AT THE CLUE PAGES,
ADD AN EXTRA 4 POINTS.

POINTS_____

TOTAL SCORE
CASE #3_____

The Kidnapped Prizewinner

As DETECTIVE SHERWOOD HAWK rushed up the steps of 538 Valley Street, the door swung wide open.

"Hurry," said the man inside. "I'm Frank Hamilton. My wife, Claudia, is missing. This is all so horrible!"

The man led Hawk up the stairs to the main bedroom. "Just look," he said, pointing to an overturned chair and rumpled bed. A window overlooking the rear of the house was wide open.

"Control yourself," said Hawk in a calming voice. "Tell me what happened."

The man stroked his forehead nervously. "I got home from work about a half hour ago and went upstairs to change. Claudia usually takes a nap before dinner. When I entered the bedroom, the room was a mess."

Hawk walked over to the window. A ladder rested against the sill.

Hawk slowly shook his head. "It looks as though your wife may have been kidnapped. She must have been carried down the ladder."

Frank Hamilton pounded his fist. "It must have been the lottery prize we won," he exclaimed. "Someone is holding Claudia for ransom!"

Hawk's mind flashed back to a newspaper article he had read. The Hamiltons had won the Empire State lottery — the largest prize in its history. They became instant millionaires.

Hawk continued. "Who was in the house when you came home?"

"Our maid Nora was here," replied Hamilton. "So was my wife's uncle, Oliver Peck."

Hamilton paused. "Maybe that explains it."

"Explains what?" asked Hawk.

"Claudia had not seen her uncle for years. He lives about a thousand miles north of here. He showed up and asked to stay for a few days. He said he was driving through on vacation."

Suddenly a voice shrieked. "Mr. Hamilton. There is a package addressed to you. Come quickly!" Nora was calling from the living room.

The men ran down the stairs and Peck rushed in from the kitchen. The distressed maid handed Hamilton a box with his name printed on it.

As everyone looked on, Frank Hamilton slowly opened the box. Suddenly his face turned white. Inside was a lock of blond hair and a note.

"That's Claudia's hair!" cried Hamilton. Hawk snatched the note and read it.

Your wife will lose more than her hair if you do not cooperate. Have $100,000 in small bills ready by tomorrow and await instructions.

"I knew that winning the lottery would bring us trouble," moaned Hamilton.

Hawk didn't seem to hear. Instead he was studying the note. "Hmm. The letter 't' in some of the words is crossed differently. One has a slanting line. Another has a wavy line."

Hawk bit on his lip. "The writer of this note disguised the handwriting so we would not recognize who wrote it."

Then he turned to Nora. "Where were you when this box arrived?"

The maid twisted a dust cloth. "I was cleaning in the hall when I heard a sound in the living room. I turned around and saw that the box had been slipped through the mail slot."

The detective looked at Oliver Peck. "I don't know a thing," Peck said. "I was out all afternoon shopping for a new set of golf clubs and returned just before Hamilton arrived."

Silence filled the air while Sherwood Hawk studied three frightened faces. Then he gazed around the room and remained deep in thought.

Finally Hawk stared directly at Mr. Hamilton. "I think we can track down your wife," he said somberly. "Someone in this room can lead us to her."

WHAT PERSON DID HAWK ACCUSE? TRY TO SOLVE THE MYSTERY; THEN TURN TO THE NEXT PAGE.

A. eulc rehtona rof kool ot deen uoy

B. niaga revo yrt dna kcab og

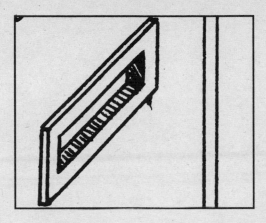

C. eciohc thgir no snoitalutargnoc

D. ecnedive tnereffid rof hcraes

AFTER YOU HAVE CHOSEN THE RIGHT CLUE, TRY TO SOLVE THE MYSTERY. THEN TURN TO THE SOLUTION TO SEE IF YOU FIGURED IT OUT.

SOLUTION

Nora, the maid, told Hawk that she was cleaning in the hall when she heard the box being slipped through the mail slot.

Hawk suddenly realized that the box was too large to fit through the slot. He knew Nora must have been lying.

The maid had hidden the box inside the house. Then, after Hawk arrived, she "produced" it and pretended it was slipped through the mail slot.

When Hawk accused Nora, the maid confessed. She and her boyfriend had plotted the crime. Her friend had kidnapped Claudia.

Nora led Hawk to the building where Claudia was being held. She was unharmed.

SCORING

If you picked the correct clue
immediately, score 3 points.

If you needed TWO clues, score 2 points.

If you needed THREE clues, score 1 point.

If you needed FOUR clues, score 0 points.

POINTS_____

DID YOU SOLVE THE CASE?
IF YOU DID, SCORE 3 POINTS.

POINTS_____

IF YOU CRACKED THE CASE *BEFORE*
YOU LOOKED AT THE CLUE PAGES,
ADD AN EXTRA 4 POINTS.

POINTS_____

TOTAL SCORE
CASE #4_____

The Carnival Car Theft

IT WAS A RELIEF TO HAVE A SUNDAY off, thought Detective Sherwood Hawk as he wandered through the noisy midway of Fernwell Carnival. After a heavy rain, the sun had finally broken through.

Hawk stopped at a booth marked BREAK-A-PLATE. Behind the counter was a row of glass plates.

"Try your skill and win!" shouted the man inside the booth, holding up a baseball. "Break a plate in two throws and win a stuffed animal."

Hawk tossed a dollar on the counter and grabbed a ball.

"Sharpening your aim?" asked a familiar voice. When Hawk turned around, there was Lester Hooper, the carnival security guard.

As Hawk wound up, a woman ran up to the guard. "My car is missing from the parking lot!" she cried. "It must have been stolen."

The woman said her name was Rhonda Figg and motioned for the guard to follow. Hawk was right behind.

They reached a row of cars and the woman pointed to an empty space. "There! I was parked between these two cars."

"Where are your car keys?" asked Hawk.

"Just who are you?" said Figg skeptically.

"This is Sherwood Hawk," answered the guard. "He's the sharpest detective in the division."

Figg reached into her dungarees pocket. "My keys are gone. Someone must have stolen them!"

Hawk nodded knowingly. "That explains a lot. There has been a string of car thefts all month. We think it is the work of an organized gang."

Hawk paused and then continued. "Was your car a new two-door Ocelot with a sunroof?"

Figg jerked back her head in surprise. "How did you know? Did you see me park?"

A slight smile crossed Hawk's face. "No. But the thieves are on the lookout for new cars. They especially target that model."

Figg ran her fingers through her hair. "Oh, please! You must find my car!"

After Figg described her Ocelot, Hawk grabbed a nearby pay phone and dialed headquarters. "Post a squad car at the main intersection of Arsdale Highway. Be on the lookout for a new white Ocelot heading west. License plate 28K902. I'll be there in twenty minutes."

Then Hawk exited the carnival grounds and sped six miles on the muddy dirt road before turning onto a main highway. Fifteen minutes later he arrived at the checkpoint.

As Sherwood Hawk pulled up, he was met by

35

a policeman. "Not much luck, Detective Hawk," said the officer. "We stopped one car. But the license plate doesn't match."

Hawk strolled over to the car. The driver was standing next to it. "What's this all about?" protested the man angrily. "I'm late for a meeting at my office."

Hawk looked at the man suspiciously. "Do you always work on Sundays?"

"Not usually," answered the driver. "But today I have an important appointment."

Hawk slowly circled the car. It matched the details of Figg's stolen Ocelot. But the license plate was different. "I'd like to see your ownership card," he asked.

The man thumbed through his wallet and looked slightly embarrassed. "Umm. I was in such a hurry to get to the office that I must have left it at home," he said sheepishly.

"Do you think we should let him get to his appointment?" asked the policeman.

Hawk stared silently at the ground as he listened to the policeman's question. Then he jerked up his head. "No, I don't think so."

"Officer," Hawk said, pointing a finger at the driver. "I want you to arrest him for stealing this Ocelot."

HOW DID HAWK KNOW? TRY TO SOLVE THE MYSTERY; THEN TURN TO THE NEXT PAGE.

A. krow doog esac eht sevlos siht

B. dael retteb a dnif tcerroc ton

C. rewsna gnorw eht dekcip uoy

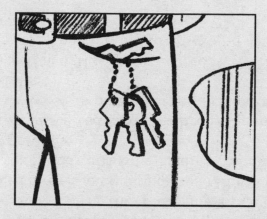

D. redrah yrt retteb tub dab oot

AFTER YOU HAVE CHOSEN THE RIGHT
CLUE, TRY TO SOLVE THE MYSTERY.
THEN TURN TO THE SOLUTION TO SEE IF
YOU FIGURED IT OUT.

SOLUTION

Hawk noticed that the car was splattered with mud, but the license plate was perfectly clean. He reasoned that the plate must have been changed *after* it left a muddy road. It could have been the muddy dirt road leading from the carnival grounds.

Hawk suspected that the license plates had been switched to disguise the fact that the car was stolen.

Inspection of the Ocelot proved it was Rhonda Figg's car. The man broke down and confessed to the car theft.

SCORING

If you picked the correct clue
immediately, score 3 points.

If you needed TWO clues, score 2 points.

If you needed THREE clues, score 1 point.

If you needed FOUR clues, score 0 points.

POINTS_____

DID YOU SOLVE THE CASE?
IF YOU DID, SCORE 3 POINTS.

POINTS_____

IF YOU CRACKED THE CASE *BEFORE*
YOU LOOKED AT THE CLUE PAGES,
ADD AN EXTRA 4 POINTS.

POINTS_____

TOTAL SCORE
CASE #5_____

The Elevator Mystery

As DARKNESS FELL ON THE CITY, DE-
tective Sherwood Hawk entered the lobby of the
Omni Building. He headed for the computer store.

The Omni was thirty-two stories high, the
tallest office building in town. Small stores lined
the spacious lobby.

"I need some computer disks," said Hawk.

"You got here just in time," answered the
clerk. "We're ready to close."

As the clerk reached into a display cabinet, a
loud scream was heard outside the store. Hawk
turned and quickly dashed into the lobby.

A short, heavyset woman was yelling at the
top of her lungs. "Randy! Randy!" A little girl,
holding a bag of jelly beans, clung to her dress.

Sherwood Hawk approached the woman and
flashed his detective badge. "Calm down," he
said. "What's wrong?"

"It's my little boy, Randy. I can't find him
anywhere!" she exclaimed.

Hawk carefully surveyed the marble floor of
the deserted lobby. Most of the shoppers had left.

Then the detective turned to the woman. "Is
Randy wearing new sneakers? And is he eating
a chocolate ice-cream cone?"

The startled woman nodded her head. "Oh, you found him!"

"No," replied Hawk. "But I think I know the direction he was headed." Hawk pointed to the middle elevator.

The detective glanced at a dripping trail of chocolate ice cream that led to the elevator. "These are Randy's footprints in the ice-cream drops. Each print is clear-cut and uniform. That's why I thought he was wearing new sneakers."

Hawk stood up and glanced at the little girl. "From the size of Randy's footprints, I would guess he is the same age as his sister. Is he?"

"You're right!" replied the woman, looking down at her daughter Audrey. "Randy is her twin brother."

Then a horrible thought seemed to strike the mother. "Oh, no! I hope Randy didn't go up to the roof. We were there only an hour ago to look down over the city. Randy begged to stay until dark so he could see it at night."

The woman gasped, realizing what that could mean. "Randy might climb over the guard rail. He could slip and fall off the building!"

"Follow me," remarked Hawk as he hurriedly walked toward the elevator.

The woman interrupted. "I just realized something," she said. "Randy could have gone down to the basement health club instead. We visited

there, too. It has a large swimming pool.

"We sat on the side and dangled our bare feet in the water. I had to promise Randy ice cream to get him to leave."

Hawk frowned. "That might be real trouble. The pool is closed and the lights are out. If Randy wanders into the dark health club, he could easily fall into the water. We don't have a minute to spare."

"But we can't check out both places at once," stammered the woman. "Time is important. We must find Randy as quickly as we can."

The mother followed Hawk into the elevator with Audrey trailing behind.

As he was about to go up to the roof, Hawk glanced at the little girl. She was standing in the corner, quietly chewing a jelly bean.

Hawk hesitated before pushing a button. "On second thought, I am certain Randy is not on the roof."

. The mother gave Hawk a puzzled look. "What do you mean?" she asked. "Where is my Randy?"

"Trust me," the detective replied. "Randy is *not* on the roof."

Hawk pressed the basement button. "If we hurry, we can catch Randy before he wanders into the pool."

HOW DID HAWK KNOW? TRY TO SOLVE THE MYSTERY; THEN TURN TO THE NEXT PAGE.

A. ecnedive rehto rof redrah hcraes

B. daetsni eulc wen a no ediced

C. rewsna tcerroc eht ton si siht

D. tuo ti erugif won uoy rof doog

AFTER YOU HAVE CHOSEN THE RIGHT CLUE, TRY TO SOLVE THE MYSTERY. THEN TURN TO THE SOLUTION TO SEE IF YOU FIGURED IT OUT.

SOLUTION

When Hawk looked at Randy's twin sister Audrey, he saw that she was too short to reach the top elevator button. Randy could not possibly have pressed it to take the elevator up to the roof.

Randy was found in the health club, sitting on a bicycle and licking his ice-cream cone.

SCORING

If you picked the correct clue
immediately, score 3 points.

If you needed TWO clues, score 2 points.

If you needed THREE clues, score 1 point.

If you needed FOUR clues, score 0 points.

POINTS_____

DID YOU SOLVE THE CASE?
IF YOU DID, SCORE 3 POINTS.

POINTS_____

IF YOU CRACKED THE CASE *BEFORE*
YOU LOOKED AT THE CLUE PAGES,
ADD AN EXTRA 4 POINTS.

POINTS_____

TOTAL SCORE
CASE #6_____

The Big Money Switch

DETECTIVE SHERWOOD HAWK GLANCED through his office window at an uprooted tree lying across the lawn. High, gusting winds had whipped through the town during the night.

As he stood up for a closer look, the phone on his desk rang. It was Sergeant Winslow.

"There is a young man out here named Wilford Pigeon. He works at Drexel's Shoe Store and says he has been robbed."

Hawk's ears perked up. "Send him in!"

A nervous young man entered and stood directly in front of Hawk's desk. Beads of sweat covered his forehead.

Wilford dropped a cloth bag on Hawk's desk. "The store's money that was inside here has been stolen!" said Wilford. "I'm sure Mr. Drexel will fire me."

Then he untied the bag and pulled out some rocks and a newspaper. "Someone switched the money for this!" he exclaimed.

"But how could it have happened?" asked Hawk.

The young man gained his composure. "You see, Mr. Drexel left the store a little early yesterday. He asked me to deposit the store's money in the bank after we closed."

"And did you?" asked Hawk inquisitively.

"That's just it," continued Wilford. "I worked very late and the bank was closed. So I took the bag to my apartment overnight.

"I returned to the bank this morning. And when I opened the bag, that is what I found." Wilford pointed to the items on Hawk's desk.

"I telephoned Mr. Drexel and told him to meet me here. It's his day off."

Hawk motioned to a chair and Wilford stiffly sat down. "So you had the money bag in your apartment all evening?" said Hawk.

"Yes," Wilford Pigeon nodded hesitantly. "But I went out for a walk about nine o'clock and got back just before the big windstorm started."

"Is it possible that someone broke into your apartment while you were out?" Hawk asked.

Wilford paused. "I guess so. Maybe a burglar replaced the money with rocks and newspaper so I wouldn't suspect anything until today."

As Hawk examined a rock, the door to his office swung open. A heavyset man barged in. He was wearing shorts and a dirty T-shirt.

"How could this have happened?" Ivan Drexel blurted at Wilford. "There was almost a thousand dollars in the bag when I gave it to you."

While Wilford sheepishly tried to explain,

Hawk drummed his fingers on the desk. "How long has Wilford been working for you?" he asked Drexel.

"About two years. I even promoted him to store manager. But there is no excuse for this!"

The detective glanced at Wilford. "Did you start working for Mr. Drexel after you quit your job at the docks?"

Wilford Pigeon gave Hawk a startled look. "How did you know I had been a longshoreman?"

Hawk calmly returned the look. "Before you left the bank you retied the bag with a very unusual knot. It is a cross running knot, I believe. Cargo handlers use it to load ships in port."

"What are you waiting for?" interrupted Drexel. "I want you to arrest Pigeon!"

"I'm just thinking," said Hawk, leaning back in his chair. "Maybe you put the rocks and newspaper inside the bag before you gave it to Wilford. You could have faked the theft to collect insurance money."

"Me?" barked Drexel. "How dare you!"

Hawk snapped his fingers and then leaned forward. "In fact, I am certain that one of you switched the money."

The detective pounded his desk. "And that person is guilty of grand larceny!"

WHICH PERSON DID HAWK ACCUSE? TRY TO SOLVE THE MYSTERY; THEN TURN TO THE NEXT PAGE.

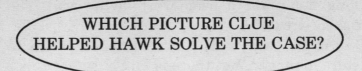

WHICH PICTURE CLUE
HELPED HAWK SOLVE THE CASE?

A. tcerroc ton si siht redrah yrt

B. eciohc tnereffid a tuo krow

C. tuo ti erugif won rewsna thgir

D. eno rehtona ot hctiws retteb uoy

AFTER YOU HAVE CHOSEN THE RIGHT
CLUE, TRY TO SOLVE THE MYSTERY.
THEN TURN TO THE SOLUTION TO SEE IF
YOU FIGURED IT OUT.

SOLUTION

Hawk noticed the headline on the newspaper. It had a story about the heavy windstorm that whipped through the town during the night. It had to be the next morning's newspaper.

The paper must have been put into the bag that morning. Only one person could have done it — Wilford Pigeon.

Before he went to the bank, Wilford had switched the money for the rocks and paper.

But he thoughtlessly used the morning's newspaper.

SCORING

If you picked the correct clue
immediately, score 3 points.

If you needed TWO clues, score 2 points.

If you needed THREE clues, score 1 point.

If you needed FOUR clues, score 0 points.

POINTS_____

DID YOU SOLVE THE CASE?
IF YOU DID, SCORE 3 POINTS.

POINTS_____

IF YOU CRACKED THE CASE *BEFORE*
YOU LOOKED AT THE CLUE PAGES,
ADD AN EXTRA 4 POINTS.

POINTS_____

TOTAL SCORE
CASE #7_____

The School Yard Vandals

"NOT AGAIN," MUMBLED A WEARY DEtective Sherwood Hawk as he approached the house next to Sheridan School playground.

It was Mr. Bumpers's third call to police headquarters. "I can't believe the children in the school yard really are bothering him," Hawk moaned. "I guess he just doesn't like kids."

The detective rang the bell. No answer. Then he pushed the doorbell again, giving it a long ring. Finally the door swung open.

There was Mr. Bumpers, a short, pudgy man. A wad of cotton was sticking out of each ear. He frowned when he saw the detective.

"This time they've gone too far," protested Bumpers as Hawk entered. "It's no use warning those kids anymore. I want them arrested immediately!"

Detective Hawk gave Bumpers a puzzled stare. "What happened?" he asked.

Bumpers stared back at the detective but didn't answer. Then he pulled out the cotton from his right ear as Hawk repeated his question in a louder voice. "WHAT HAPPENED?"

"No need to shout," snapped the man. "I can hear you perfectly well without the cotton. It's those kids in the school yard again. They were tossing a baseball.

"It was Seth Webster and Kennie Hopkins. One of them threw it right through my window."

Hawk gazed at the double windows across the room. One of the glass panes was broken. A baseball lay on the rug.

"Those kids are driving me crazy," said Bumpers. "Every time I come into this room I hear their howling and hooting."

Hawk walked over and examined the broken pane. Then he pushed open one side of the windows and scanned the empty school yard.

"This time I believe you," said Hawk angrily. "At first I thought you were exaggerating the loud noise."

Hawk walked back to the center of the room. "When did this happen?" he asked.

"About a half hour ago," replied Bumpers. "I was relaxing in my chair. When they began making noise, I stuffed some cotton in my ears. Suddenly a ball crashed through the window."

As Bumpers was speaking, Hawk picked up a book lying on top of the TV. He glanced at the cover and then replaced it.

"I guess they interrupted you while you were watching cartoons," he said.

Bumpers gave Hawk a surprised look. "What makes you think I like cartoons?"

Hawk paused. "Your television dial is on

channel four. This time of day the channel has an hour-long cartoon show."

Bumpers seemed a little sheepish. "Oh, it was turned to channel four from last night. That's when I was watching bowling."

Hawk shook his head. "I don't think so. The TV felt warm when I touched it. You must have turned it off just before I arrived."

Bumpers's face turned red in embarrassment. "Well . . . sometimes I watch cartoons. But only when nothing else is on.

"But never mind what I watch," barked Bumpers. "Do something about those kids!"

Hawk frowned. "I'll go over to the principal's office and get the boys out of class."

Hawk started to leave, then suddenly he stopped short in his tracks. "Just one more question," he said. "How do I know you didn't fake this whole thing?"

Bumpers's face stiffened. "Me?" he asked.

Hawk crossed his arms and looked sternly at Bumpers. "Maybe you did it so I would pull the kids out of class and scare them.

"In fact, I'm sure the boys didn't break your window. I think you did it yourself."

HOW DID HAWK KNOW? TRY TO SOLVE THE MYSTERY; THEN TURN TO THE NEXT PAGE.

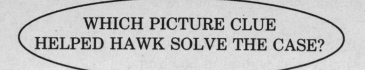

WHICH PICTURE CLUE
HELPED HAWK SOLVE THE CASE?

A. siht morf eno tnereffid a dnif

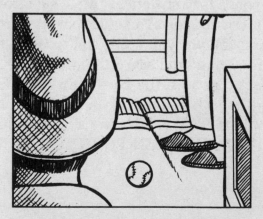

B. gniyrt peek noisiced gnorw

C. eciohc siht htiw pu deppils uoy

D. esac eht evlos og ti tog uoy

AFTER YOU HAVE CHOSEN THE RIGHT
CLUE, TRY TO SOLVE THE MYSTERY.
THEN TURN TO THE SOLUTION TO SEE IF
YOU FIGURED IT OUT.

SOLUTION

Hawk noticed that all the broken glass was on the *outside* sill. Since the windows were closed when he arrived, the pane was smashed from inside the den.

Trapped by the evidence, Mr. Bumpers admitted he grabbed a baseball and smashed the pane of glass.

Then he pulled the wad of cotton out of his other ear and meekly apologized to Sherwood Hawk.

SCORING

If you picked the correct clue
immediately, score 3 points.

If you needed TWO clues, score 2 points.

If you needed THREE clues, score 1 point.

If you needed FOUR clues, score 0 points.

POINTS_____

DID YOU SOLVE THE CASE?
IF YOU DID, SCORE 3 POINTS.

POINTS_____

IF YOU CRACKED THE CASE *BEFORE*
YOU LOOKED AT THE CLUE PAGES,
ADD AN EXTRA 4 POINTS.

POINTS_____

TOTAL SCORE
CASE #8 _____

The Factory Fire

IT WAS LATE FRIDAY AFTERNOON AS A large crowd gathered outside the Dornbush Shoe Factory. Roaring flames shot out from the windows, fanned by whipping winds.

Detective Sherwood Hawk wound his way through the onlookers. Carefully sidestepping the maze of fire hoses, he moved closer to the building. Smoke was billowing everywhere.

A large empty trash drum stood next to the burning building. On the top of the pile of rubbish lay a crumpled sheet of newspaper.

As the firefighters called out to each other, Hawk opened the paper and quickly scanned the page. It was Wednesday's paper. Strange, he thought. The garbage was emptied daily. Why was a two-day-old newspaper on top?

Hawk gazed at an article near the bottom of the page. It was a three-day weather forecast.

Suddenly Hawk stiffened. Instantly he knew that the fire was set on purpose. And the newspaper had been tossed in the trash by the arsonist.

Hawk angrily clenched his teeth. The fire had been planned very carefully. The arsonist needed to choose a day with strong winds so that the fire would spread quickly. And the weather forecast predicted that this was the day.

A small dark stain in the corner of the paper confirmed Hawk's suspicion. It had the distinctive smell of gasoline!

Hawk curiously scanned the faces of the on-looking crowd.

Abruptly Hawk's gaze stopped at Perry Bond. He recognized him as the owner of a shoe factory in the same town. Hawk remembered that Bond and Dornbush were bitter rivals. Could Bond have had something to do with the fire?

Hawk walked over and tapped Bond on the shoulder. "Can I speak to you for a moment?"

A startled Bond turned around. "What's wrong?" he asked.

Bond followed Hawk across the street. "I guess you are not too unhappy about this fire," said Hawk.

The man looked nervously at the detective. "What are you getting at!' he snapped.

"I'm just asking you a question," Hawk casually replied. "When did you get here?"

"I was on my way home when I noticed the heavy smell of smoke." Bond motioned at his parked car. "I could smell it from blocks away.

"I got here just before the fire trucks arrived," Bond continued. "Do you think the fire was set on purpose?"

Before Hawk could answer, Bond pointed to a

bearded man in the crowd. "I think you should check out the guy over there. I saw him standing outside the building when I arrived."

Hawk pushed through the crowd and returned, followed by the bearded onlooker. He identified himself as Adam Scudder and was wearing soiled dungarees.

"This man claims you were near the factory just after the fire started," said Hawk.

"That's right," Scudder declared. "My house is a half mile east of here. I was in my backyard, on the lounge chair, when I sensed the smell of smoke in the air. So I ran out to find out where it came from. I was the first person on the scene."

Hawk listened carefully, wondering what the man looked like without his beard. He seemed vaguely familiar. "Did you call the fire department?" Hawk asked.

Scudder shook his head. "I heard the building's fire alarm go off just as I arrived. So I knew that help was on the way."

Hawk looked at both men suspiciously. Could either of them have started the fire?

Then Hawk grabbed one by the arm. "I want you to accompany me to police headquarters."

The detective tightened his grip. "I think you had something to do with starting this fire."

WHICH PERSON DID HAWK ACCUSE? TRY TO SOLVE THE MYSTERY; THEN TURN TO THE NEXT PAGE.

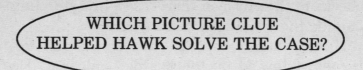

WHICH PICTURE CLUE
HELPED HAWK SOLVE THE CASE?

A. rewsna rehtona tuo kees

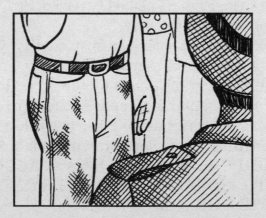

B. eno tcerroc eht ton si siht

C. eulc thgir eht dekcip uoy boj ecin

D. eulc siht no deloof tog uoy

AFTER YOU HAVE CHOSEN THE RIGHT
CLUE, TRY TO SOLVE THE MYSTERY.
THEN TURN TO THE SOLUTION TO SEE IF
YOU FIGURED IT OUT.

SOLUTION

It was late in the afternoon when the factory was aflame. Hawk realized that the strong winds were blowing the flames toward the west, the same direction as the sun, which sets in the west.

Scudder claimed that he sensed the smell of smoke while he was in his yard. But Scudder said he lived *east* of the factory. He would not have been able to smell the smoke in his backyard. It would have blown in the opposite direction.

Scudder confessed to starting the fire. A check of police files showed that he had been found guilty of burning another building four years earlier.

SCORING

If you picked the correct clue
immediately, score 3 points.

If you needed TWO clues, score 2 points.

If you needed THREE clues, score 1 point.

If you needed FOUR clues, score 0 points.

POINTS_____

DID YOU SOLVE THE CASE?
IF YOU DID, SCORE 3 POINTS.

POINTS_____

IF YOU CRACKED THE CASE *BEFORE*
YOU LOOKED AT THE CLUE PAGES,
ADD AN EXTRA 4 POINTS.

POINTS_____

TOTAL SCORE
CASE #9_____

The Missing Statue

As DETECTIVE SHERWOOD HAWK'S CAR pulled up to 42 Elm Street, a tall, gray-haired woman wearing an apron rushed toward him.

"Hurry, come inside," she exclaimed. "There has been a robbery. It's all so terrible!"

Hawk followed her through the front door and into the kitchen. "You'll be okay," said Hawk reassuringly. "Just settle down."

"I'm Etta, the housekeeper," the agitated woman explained. "Someone stole Mrs. Tuttle's antique statue from its stand in the hallway. She will be furious!"

Hawk noticed an empty pedestal in the hallway beyond the kitchen. "Tell me exactly what happened," he said.

Etta took a deep breath. "I returned from the supermarket about an hour ago. A thief broke in while I was gone. He was hiding in the house when I returned.

"I put away the groceries and began making dinner before Mr. and Mrs. Tuttle got home. The thief must have hidden in the hallway closet."

The shaken housekeeper continued. "I was mixing the salad when I heard a noise behind me. I turned around and there he was, trying to slip out the back door. The statue was under his arm."

"What did he look like?" asked Hawk.

"His back was to me, so I couldn't see his face," answered Etta. "But I hit him," she said proudly.

Hawk's eyes widened. "What do you mean?"

"I threw a bottle of vinegar at his head," explained Etta. "It must have hit him hard because he yelled as he darted out the door."

Hawk gazed near the door and saw a pool of pink liquid with an empty vinegar bottle beside it. He kneeled down. It smelled like vinegar.

Hawk rose to face Etta. "Did you touch anything after the thief ran out?"

"Not a thing," replied the housekeeper, shaking her head.

Hawk carefully considered her answer. "Let me see if I have this right. The thief tried to sneak out the kitchen door behind your back?"

"Yes." She nodded in agreement. "He couldn't use the front door without being seen. Our next door neighbor is outside mowing his lawn."

"Did he take anything else?" asked Hawk.

"Nothing!" Etta replied emphatically. "I checked the entire house."

"I guess that Mr. and Mrs. Tuttle will be back soon," declared Hawk. "It is almost dinnertime and they will want to get ready before their four friends arrive."

The housekeeper looked surprised. "But how

did you know there are four guests for dinner?"

Hawk pointed at the glasses on the kitchen counter. "There are six water glasses, so it must be the Tuttles and four friends."

"How could you know they are friends and not business guests?"

Hawk stroked his chin thoughtfully. "I see the table is set in the kitchen. And with paper napkins. No, it couldn't be a fancy dinner or it would have been in the dining room. It must be a casual dinner with friends."

Hawk's slight smile disappeared. "Was the statue very valuable?"

"My, yes," replied Etta. "Mrs. Tuttle bought it at an auction several months ago. I dust it very carefully."

Hawk paused for a moment and then stared skeptically at Etta. "Your story sounds very suspicious. You know, I think you knocked over the statue while you were dusting it and faked the theft to cover up the accident."

"What do you mean?" insisted Etta, raising her voice. "If I hadn't come back from the supermarket when I did, the crook could have cleaned out this entire house."

"Let's wait for the Tuttles," continued Hawk. "You tell them what really happened."

HOW DID HAWK KNOW? TRY TO SOLVE THE MYSTERY; THEN TURN TO THE NEXT PAGE.

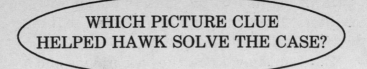

WHICH PICTURE CLUE
HELPED HAWK SOLVE THE CASE?

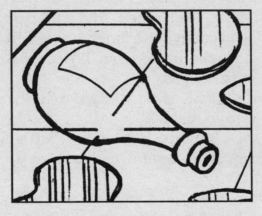

A. ti tog uoy gnikniht tnellecxe

B. thgir ton si siht tub dab oot

C. niaga yrt redrah kniht tsum uoy

D. eciohc tnereffid a retfa og

AFTER YOU HAVE CHOSEN THE RIGHT CLUE, TRY TO SOLVE THE MYSTERY. THEN TURN TO THE SOLUTION TO SEE IF YOU FIGURED IT OUT.

SOLUTION

Hawk noticed the vinegar bottle that Etta said she had thrown. It was completely empty and the pink vinegar had spilled out on the floor. He immediately knew that Etta had made up the story.

Because of the round shape of the bottle and its long neck, it would be impossible for *all* of the vinegar to drain out, even if it had been thrown at the thief. Some vinegar would have remained inside the bottle.

Etta had staged the crime. She emptied the bottle onto the floor and placed it beside the pool of vinegar to suggest she threw it at the thief.

Caught by her mistake, Etta confessed to Hawk. While she was dusting, she had accidentally knocked over the statue and broken it.

SCORING

If you picked the correct clue
immediately, score 3 points.

If you needed TWO clues, score 2 points.

If you needed THREE clues, score 1 point.

If you needed FOUR clues, score 0 points.

POINTS_____

DID YOU SOLVE THE CASE?
IF YOU DID, SCORE 3 POINTS.

POINTS_____

IF YOU CRACKED THE CASE *BEFORE*
YOU LOOKED AT THE CLUE PAGES,
ADD AN EXTRA 4 POINTS.

POINTS_____

TOTAL SCORE
CASE #10_____

HOW GOOD A DETECTIVE ARE YOU?

List your score here:

Case $\dfrac{}{1}$ + $\dfrac{}{2}$ + $\dfrac{}{3}$ + $\dfrac{}{4}$ + $\dfrac{}{5}$ = _____

Case $\dfrac{}{6}$ + $\dfrac{}{7}$ + $\dfrac{}{8}$ + $\dfrac{}{9}$ + $\dfrac{}{10}$ = _____

TOTAL SCORE _____

SCORE

76–100 points. . . . . . Master Detective

50–75 points. . . . Investigator First Class

30–49 points. . . . . . . Amateur Sleuth

below 30 points. . . Rookie Beat Policeman

NOTES

NOTES

NOTES